This vacation Bible school inspired the
Bible Buddy named Skyler. Skyler is a
bowerbird. In God's creation, bowerbirds
are real makers who build amazing dens
filled with flowers, shells,
and colorful stones.

How cool is that?

**Best of Buddies
Uh-Oh! I Did It Again!**

Written by **JEFF WHITE**   *Illustrated by* **DAVID HARRINGTON**

Copyright © 2017 Group Publishing, Inc./ISNI: 0000 0001 0362 4853
Lifetree is an imprint of Group Publishing, Inc.
group.com

Library of Congress Cataloging-in-Publications Data on file.

ISBN: 978-1-4707-4854-8 (Hard Cover)
ISBN: 978-1-4707-5022-0 (e Pub)
Printed in China. 001 CHINA 0617

10 9 8 7 6 5 4 3 2 1   21 20 19 18 17

Uh-oh! I did it again!

Written by **JEFF WHITE**   Illustrated by **DAVID HARRINGTON**

Skyler loves to make things.

He's a builder, a creator,

a crafter, and an inventor.

BUT...

Somehow, some way,

Skyler almost always makes a mess.

Skyler cleans up the milk.

Everything is sparkly!

Ooooooooo.

But watch out for the...

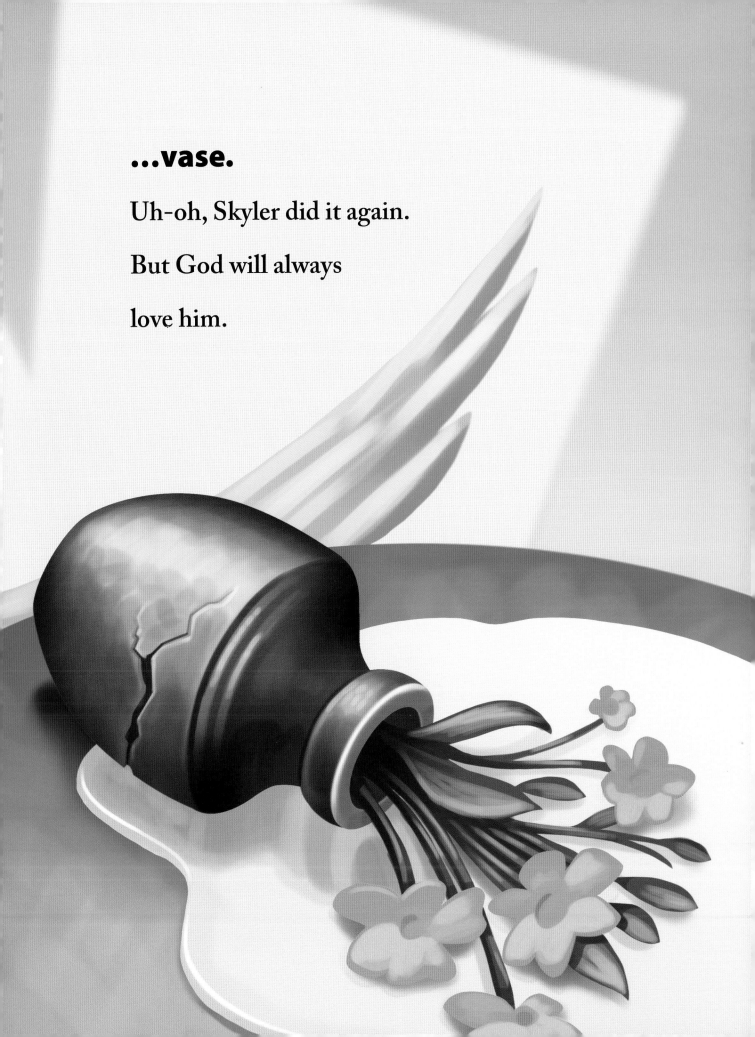

...vase.

Uh-oh, Skyler did it again.

But God will always

love him.

He gives the flowers a new drink. Aaaahhhhh.

But watch out for the...

**...fishbowl.**

Uh-oh, Skyler did it again.

But God will always

love him.

Skyler makes a new home for the fish.

Yaaaaaaaaay!

But watch out for the...

...picture frame.

Uh-oh, that clumsy bird did it again.

But God will always love him.

He makes the frame as good as new.

(Kind of.) Lovely! Awwwwwww.

But watch out for the...

...watermelon.

Uh-oh, he did it again.

But God will always love him.

Look at that merry melon. Wow!

But watch out for the...

...lamp.

Uh-oh, Skyler did it again.

But God will always love him.

The lamp is shining bright again.

Woo-hoo!

But watch out for the...

...broom.

Uh-oh, our happy friend did it again. But God will always, always love him.

Skyler spent the day making some new things…

and making other things new.

He learned sometimes

broken things can

become even better.

And, above all, he knows one thing is true.

God will always love him!

And God will always love you!